MARVEL
SPIDER-MAN

ADVENTURES OF THE
WEB-SLINGER

Written by Simon Hugo

Editorial Assistant Beth Davies
Designer Sam Bartlett
Senior Editor Hannah Dolan
Pre-Production Producer Marc Staples
Producer Isabell Schart
Managing Editor Paula Regan
Managing Art Editor Guy Harvey
Art Director Lisa Lanzarini
Publisher Julie Ferris
Publishing Director Simon Beecroft

Reading Consultant Maureen Fernandes

The author would like to thank Ned Hartley and Mark McKenzie-Ray
for their assistance.

First published in 2016 in Great Britain by Dorling Kindersley Limited
80 Strand, London, WC2R 0RL
A Penguin Random House Company

10 9 8 7 6 5 4 3 2 1

001–291444–Apr/2016

marvelkids.com

©2016 MARVEL

A CIP catalogue record for this book
is available from the British Library.

ISBN: 978-0-24124-965-9

Printed and bound in China.

www.dk.com

A WORLD OF IDEAS
SEE ALL THERE IS TO KNOW

Contents

Introduction

Spider-Man is the friendly neighbourhood hero with the powers of a super spider. He can climb up walls, spin sticky webs and swing between buildings without even breaking a sweat. He uses his powers to fight crime and to save people who are in danger.

Spider-Man wears a mask to stop his enemies from finding out who he really is. Only a handful of his closest friends and fellow Super Heroes know that his real name is Peter Parker – and that underneath the mask there is a young man trying to live an ordinary life.

There is nothing ordinary about Peter's life, however. Ever since he was bitten by a radioactive spider, he has been the hero at the heart of one amazing adventure after another. He has super strength and speed, but he also has a brilliant brain, and likes to use his scientific skills whenever he can.

If he sets out to stop a Super Villain's plot,
the bad guys should fear Peter's mind as
much as Spidey's muscles.

Spider-Man has many friends and many
enemies. He has battled monsters and saved
the world from Super Villains. He has made
tough choices and lost loved ones. His story
is far from over, but these are some of the
best parts so far...

Peter Parker

Life at Midtown High School was tough for young Peter Parker. Although Peter loved to study, especially science, he was shy and found it difficult to make friends. He was not strong or good at sports, and some of his classmates called him "Puny Parker". No one wished they had super-powers more than Peter!

Peter lived with his Aunt May and Uncle Ben. His mother and father had died a long time ago, and he was too young to remember much about them.

Peter loved his aunt and uncle very much, and they cared for him more than anyone else in the world. They encouraged Peter in his studies, and were always there to comfort him after a tough day at school. Peter hoped that his life would be different one day – but that Aunt May and Uncle Ben would never change!

SCHOOL REPORT

Peter is a highly intelligent individual. However, his school report card shows he has his strengths and weaknesses – just like everyone else.

M H S Midtown High School
· REPORT CARD ·

NAME: Peter Parker

YEAR: 11

TEACHER: Raymond Warren

CLASS: A-15

TEACHER'S NOTES:

Peter is a bright boy, who excels in Maths and Science. He also has a strong creative flair – photography is clearly a passion for him. Peter is a quiet member of the class, who sometimes struggles with confidence. If Peter can improve his self-confidence, he will go far.

Raymond Warren

CLASS	GRADE	NOTES
MATHS	A+	With his grasp of complex systems, Peter could become a web designer.
ENGLISH	A	Peter loves to read – especially comics. It's a shame his handwriting is so spidery.
SCIENCE	A+	Peter's best subject! If he keeps this up, he will win a place at university.
ART	B	Peter's flair for photography is matched by his talent for costume design.
SPORTS	F	Mr Parker will never be an athlete. He has all the strength of a little bug!

No matter what else was happening (or
not happening) in Peter's life, he still loved
his studies. Finding out about the wonders
of science was his way of escaping from the
everyday world. So when he heard about an
event called "Experiments in Radioactivity",
he had to see what it was all about.

The event was held in a real laboratory, where scientists were showing off the power of radioactive rays. No one saw when a tiny spider got in the way of one of the rays. The unlucky spider was now radioactive, and it reacted to the shock in the only way it knew how: by biting the nearest living thing!

Peter Parker was the nearest living thing, and he began to feel very strange straight away. On his way home, he was nearly hit by a passing car. When he jumped to avoid it, he went further than he had ever jumped before. In fact, he had landed halfway up the side of a tall building!

Peter felt confused by the strange things that were happening to him. His whole body was bursting with energy, and he could climb up walls just as easily as he could walk down a street. When he crushed a metal pipe in his hand without even trying, he realised that the spider's bite had changed him. He had been given amazing powers!

Peter soon started to think about what he could use his awesome new abilities for. He realised that his days of being "Puny Parker" were at an end and that no one would be able to laugh at him any more. The unbelievable powers that had alarmed him at first could be his ticket to fame and fortune. He would make himself a spider suit and invent a way to spin his own webs. He would become a Spider-Man!

Peter wanted a real test of his strength and speed, so he put on a mask and entered a contest to fight with a powerful wrestler. A big crowd watched as Peter won the fight easily, and it wasn't long before he was given the chance to show off his skills on TV.

For his first television appearance, Peter dressed in his full spider suit and gave the audience a glimpse of just what he could do with his homemade web shooters. He didn't want to use his powers for a good reason. He just wanted to be famous.

Spider-Man's TV show was an instant hit and everyone wanted to see more. As Peter left the TV studio, he had to deal with talent scouts and newspaper reporters who all wanted to talk to the man inside the spider suit.

But they were not the only people that Peter saw backstage. He also came face-to-face with a thief who was running away from a security guard. Peter had the chance to stop him, but he let him get away. He was sick of having problems to deal with. From now on, he just wanted an easy life.

Spider-Man became a celebrity after his first TV appearance, and Peter was kept busy putting on shows for adoring fans. Though his success had gone to his head, he still thought of his Aunt May and Uncle Ben. He promised himself that he would do all he could to make them both happy and support them as they had supported him.

One day, after a successful Spidey show, Peter came home to terrible news. Uncle Ben was dead. A burglar had broken into their home and Ben had surprised him. A police officer told Peter where the burglar was hiding out and Peter didn't even wait to see Aunt May. He threw on his Spider-Man suit and went to find the guilty man.

Peter tracked down the burglar and beat him easily in a fight. He was shocked to see that it was the same man who had run past him at the TV studio. If Peter had stopped the thief when he first had the chance, his Uncle Ben would still be alive.

After the death of his uncle, Peter had to face up to what being a hero really meant. If he wanted to use the great powers he had been given, he had no choice but to accept great responsibility as well. His first duty was to care for his Aunt May, who needed him now more than ever. He also had to think about all the good things that he could do as a Super Hero.

Peter turned his back on TV fame and started to use his powers to fight crime. He snared small-time crooks in his web before they could cause more trouble. He even began to battle Super Villains such as the Vulture, Sandman and Doctor Octopus. Being a hero wasn't the easy life that Peter had imagined when he first put on his Spidey suit, but he knew that it was the right thing to do with his new gifts.

It was a new start for Spider-Man – but it wasn't the end for Peter Parker. In fact, his story was just beginning…

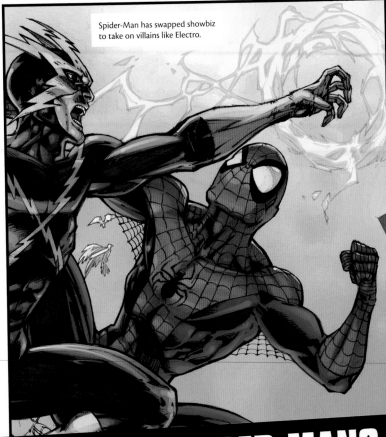
Spider-Man has swapped showbiz to take on villains like Electro.

WHO IS SPIDER-MAN?

Everyone has seen him on TV, and now he's started fighting crime. Some of us have even seen him swinging over our heads. Who is the man beneath the spider mask? We went onto the streets to see what YOU think!

A Bugle Buzz magazine SPECIAL investigation!

"He's so cool! I bet he's someone famous like... the President!"
Beth, accountant.

"He must be a crook, or why would he hide his face?"
John, publisher.

"You want to know who Spidey is? I'm Spidey!"
Flash, student.

"Whoever he is, I hope he's careful not to hurt anybody."
May, retired.

"I think he sounds like a pretty cool guy!"
Peter, student.

With Great Power...

It only took a moment for that spider to bite Peter Parker, but it took a long time for the troubled teen to fully understand the amazing powers he had been given. In fact, he's still finding out new things about himself.

Spider-Man's ability to crawl up the side of buildings takes concentration. He had to teach himself to use this power carefully, otherwise he would stick to everything! He also had to learn to master the spider-sense that alerts him to nearby danger.

At first, this spider-sense was just an odd feeling in the back of his mind, but now it is a vital part of his daily battle against crime.

One power that the spider's bite did not give Peter was the ability to spin webs. That was something he had to invent for himself, using his scientific skills to create web shooters that he can wear on his wrists.

With these skills and powers under his control, and with a cool costume to wear, Peter can be confident that when his spider-sense tingles, he will be ready for whatever adventures the day has in store for him!

SUITING UP

Peter made his Spidey suit in his bedroom.
He has added new technology to it over time,
but its main job is always to hide his true identity.

DRAWING UP
Peter sketched how he wanted his suit to look before he started to make it.

STITCHING UP
Peter made his first suit from old clothes and then added his own web pattern.

MASKING UP
A mask completed the costume, hiding Peter's face from the world.

GOING UP
Peter tested his suit by heading out for some well-dressed wall-crawling!

WEBBING UP
Web shooters small enough to fit under the suit were Peter's own invention.

STOCKING UP
Peter carries back-up packs of web fluid in his belt, along with other gadgets.

Spidey's webs are strong enough to support his weight.

Flexible boots for climbing up walls

Latest suit made from high-tech materials

The mask makes Spider-Man's voice sound deeper than Peter Parker's.

Spidey can see out of his mirrored mask, but no one can see in!

25

When Spider-Man takes on a super-powered opponent, he needs more than just the ability to climb up walls. He must use the speed and strength of a spider. That might not sound very powerful, but it is extraordinary when multiplied to match the size of a man.

Spidey can break down walls with his bare hands, bend solid metal bars and lift almost 10 tonnes – which is more than the weight of an elephant! He can also jump much further than any normal human being, leaping from one side of a street to another, or from the ground to the roof of a three-storey building.

Peter can control his strength thanks to his spider-like reflexes, which work up to 40 times faster than the brain and body of an average person.

If Spidey does suffer an injury, his super-speed even extends to healing, helping him recover from serious wounds in just a few days. It all comes in handy when battling a ferocious Super Villain such as the enormous Lizard.

Smile! Spidey might be watching. There is more to Peter Parker than just fighting crime. He also wants to live a normal life, and that means he needs a job to pay the bills. Peter is a talented photographer and takes pictures of Spider-Man that nobody else can get. Newspaper editor John Jonah Jameson hired Peter to take photographs of Spidey, not realising that the two were one and the same!

Peter's incredible pictures soon became a regular feature of the *Daily Bugle*, showing Spider-Man and his enemies in action. Peter set up cameras to take photos as he swooped by, and went back to collect the shots after he had dealt with the villains.

The only problem was that J.J. Jameson hated Spider-Man. He used Peter's photos to sell stories telling people that Spidey was a criminal. Even when Spider-Man saved the life of Jameson's son, the newspaper boss still found a way to blame the web-slinger.

Peter needed the money, so he had no choice but to go on selling his photos to the *Bugle*. He kept on looking for another way to make a living that didn't involve Spider-Man in any way.

DAILY BUGLE

Peter sells his photographs of Spider-Man to J.J. Jameson, the editor of the *Daily Bugle* newspaper. Unfortunately for Peter, J.J. hates Spidey and reports his good deeds as crimes!

DAILY 🎺 BUGLE

SPIDER-MAN
ENDANGERS CHILD'S LIFE

READ MORE INSIDE!

TERRIFIED BYSTANDERS shook with fear yesterday, as the masked menace known as "Spider-Man" terrorised the streets once more.

These EXCLUSIVE pictures show the horrific moments when the web-weaving pest endangered the lives of innocent civilians. With no care for those around him, Spider-Man flew through the air, just inches above the heads of law-abiding families and at least one sweet little old lady.

But that wasn't enough chaos for Spider-Man! He was later seen clutching a child near the infant's distraught mother. Word on the street was that Spider-Man was "saving the child from drowning", but this was clearly part of a sinister kidnapping plot!

The *Daily Bugle* has seen enough of these shocking scenes. We demand to know: who is the Spider-Man? And just who can stop his criminal rampage?

Peter's next jobs all made good use of his brilliant brain without relying on his powers as Spider-Man. First he became a science teacher at his old school, and then a teaching assistant at Empire State University. Peter really got a chance to shine when he went on a tour of Horizon Labs and impressed the scientists so much that they made him part of their team!

Horizon Labs is a state-of-the-art research centre where genius-level inventors come up with ideas for new technology. Peter made the most of his opportunity and quickly set to work building new equipment for Spider-Man to use. Nobody at the Labs realised that Peter was Spider-Man – they all thought he was just helping him.

Peter left Horizon Labs when his body was taken over by Doctor Octopus (see p.78). This Super Villain thought he could do a better job of being Spider-Man than Peter himself. He even set up a new business called Parker Industries while he was pretending to be Peter. When Peter was himself again, he found he had his own company to run!

As the boss of Parker Industries, Peter is able to carry on the work he started at Horizon Labs, finding new ways to stop Super Villains from causing havoc. As Spidey, he still finds time to teach as well – passing on his Super Hero knowledge to students at the Avengers Academy.

SUIT SCRAPBOOK

Peter has adapted his costume many times.
Each new suit is specially customised to help
Spider-Man succeed in his latest mission.

This book belongs to:

~~Peter~~ Spider-Man

This is my bulletproof
suit! I made it at
Horizon Labs when
I lost my spider-
sense for a while.

I built this armoured
outfit at university. It
looked pretty cool, but
it really slowed
me down. →

Stealth suit? What stealth suit? This outfit made me completely invisible. Though not in this picture, obviously!

I designed this suit to defeat the Sinister Six. It can withstand Rhino's strength and Electro's energy blasts.

This is the first disguise I ever wore. It's a bit basic, but it was good enough to beat this wrestler!

Terrible Foes

You can judge a Super Hero by the quality of his enemies – and Spider-Man has done battle with the best of the worst! From humans to aliens, it seems like there's always a new Super Villain to test Peter Parker's strength and skill.

When Peter first became Spider-Man, one criminal genius believed defeating the web-slinger would secure his place as the King of Crime. The man was Norman Osborn, a greedy businessman with a lust for power. He used a dangerous mix of chemicals to make himself stronger and smarter. Then he disguised himself as a monster he had seen in a nightmare. He called himself the Green Goblin.

As the Goblin, Norman tried to destroy Spider-Man, but he never succeeded and grew more insane with each failure.
Yet as Norman Osborn, he remained a respected businessman, and used his chemically boosted brainpower to convince the world that he was the true hero.

HARRY AND NORMAN

Harry Osborn is Peter Parker's friend and Norman Osborn's son. He does not get along well with his Dad, and doesn't know that Norman is really the Super Villain known as the Green Goblin.

Inbox (1)
Contacts
Favourites
Sent Mail
Drafts
Trash

From: Harry Osborn
To: Norman Osborn
Subject: Spider-Man!

Sunday 11:37

Hi Dad,

Have you seen Peter's latest photos of Spider-Man? He really showed the Green Goblin who is best!

It's funny, I feel like you've been more distant than ever since the Green Goblin came along.

It would be really great to hear from you. My friends at university think it must be great to be the son of Norman Osborn, but I wish you had an ordinary job and weren't such a rich, important businessman.

Speak soon?

Harry

Inbox (63)

Contacts

Favourites

Sent Mail

Drafts

Trash

From: Norman Osborn

To: Harry Osborn

Subject: Re: Spider-Man!

Friday 05:53

Harry,

You sound well. I am glad. But please remember that I don't have time to email you every week.

Do you mean the image attached below? Why are you sure that Spider-Man is the hero here? Does anyone even know who he is?

I advise you to read the *Daily Bugle* a little more often, if you wish to know the truth about Spider-Man.

As for your wish that I had an "ordinary job"... You really don't have anything to complain about! The more money I make, the better it is for you.

I have given you everything a son could want. If you are lucky, one day you will be just like me.

Regards,

N

39

Norman Osborn turned himself into the Green Goblin on purpose, but some Super Villains are the unlucky victims of accidents. Electro is a powerful criminal who can control electricity – draining it from cables and machines before shooting it out from his fingers and eyes. However, he was once just an ordinary man called Maxwell Dillon. Unlucky Max was struck by lightning while holding on to two power lines, leaving him buzzing with electrical energy. He realised that he could use this power as a weapon and

decided to give up his quiet life for a life of crime. Spider-Man has defeated Electro many times, but he also saved Max's life when he tried to absorb too much energy.

Just like Electro, Doctor Octopus was also created in a freak accident. But unlike Max Dillon, Otto Octavius was far from ordinary before he turned into Doc Ock.

Otto was one of the world's greatest atomic scientists. He was famous for inventing special robotic arms that let him handle dangerous materials at a safe distance. It was a chemical explosion in his laboratory that bonded him to these metal arms and gave him the power to control them with his mind.

Now that he was strong as well as clever, Doctor Octopus decided that nothing should stand in the way of his scientific research. He stole equipment and forced people to help him. He also hijacked a nuclear laboratory, and only Spider-Man was able to save the day.

When Doc Ock was sent to jail, his robot arms were taken away. Nobody knew that he could control the arms even when they weren't part of his body. He used the power of his mind to make them come and rescue him.

He grew obsessed with Spider-Man and formed a gang to work against him called the Sinister Six. He even attacked Aunt May – he kidnapped her and planned to marry her as part of his villainous plot.

THE SINISTER SIX

Doc Ock formed the Sinister Six when he realised Super Villains had to work together to bring down Spider-Man. Members have come and gone, but this latest line-up is the meanest of them all!

DOCTOR OCTOPUS

REAL NAME: Otto Octavius
POWERS: Controls his metal arms with his mind
ROLE: Doc Ock is a true criminal mastermind, and the driving force behind most of the Sinister Six's plans. His metal tentacles are the long arms of lawlessness!

MYSTERIO

REAL NAME: Quentin Beck
POWERS: Master of magic and illusion
ROLE: Mysterio delights in causing confusion wherever he goes. This makes it harder for Spider-Man to stop the Sinister Six – or even see them!

ELECTRO

REAL NAME: Maxwell Dillon
POWERS: Control over electrical energy and charges
ROLE: As a human battery, Electro adds a whole new level of power to the Sinister Six! This bright spark is the only member of the gang who has the ability to fly.

SANDMAN

REAL NAME: William Baker
POWERS: Can change his size, shape and hardness
ROLE: Sandman expands the size of the Sinister Six in more ways than one! He can make himself into a giant, or spread himself out like an army.

THE CHAMELEON

REAL NAME: Dmitri Smerdyakov
POWERS: Master of disguise and mimicry
ROLE: The Chameleon helps the Sinister Six cover their tracks, pretending to be other people and making them look guilty of crimes they did not commit.

RHINO

REAL NAME: Aleksei Sytsevich
POWERS: The speed and strength of a rhinoceros
ROLE: The Rhino is not the brains of the Sinister Six, but his brute strength and inability to feel pain make him a valuable addition to any criminal gang.

Sandman is a very different kind of villain from Doc Ock, although they both fight in the Sinister Six. He was a cheat at school and later became a crook. His real name is William Baker, but he took the nickname "Sandman" after a huge dose of radiation blended his body with the sandy ground beneath him, meaning that he could change his shape as easily as if it were sand.

The first time that Spider-Man met Sandman, he thought he was just an ordinary criminal. However, the Super Villain was able to make himself as hard as rock one minute, and then literally slip through Spider-Man's fingers the next. The web-slinger beat him by sucking him into a vacuum cleaner when he turned to tiny grains of sand – but Sandman would not fall for that trick again!

Sandman has fought Spider-Man many

times, turning his fists into huge hammers, or his whole body into a whirling sandstorm. He has sometimes tried to be good and redeem himself, but being a hero goes against his villainous grains.

It seems unlikely that Spider-Man and Sandman will ever be friends, but at times the terrifying monster known as the Lizard is one of Spidey's closest allies. That's because the Lizard lives inside Doctor Curt Connors – and sometimes the doctor has to live inside the Lizard.

Doctor Connors is a brilliant chemist who has helped Spider-Man find ways to stop some of the Super Villains he has faced. He also invented a way for humans to grow back lost body parts, just like some reptiles do. He tested it on himself to see if his missing right arm would grow back. It worked, but it also turned him into the Lizard!

The Lizard is very powerful and wants to turn everyone in the world into scaly green creatures like him. He hates Spider-Man for trying to foil his plans, and has often tried to destroy him. Spider-Man has helped turn the Lizard back into Doctor Connors, but the monster is never gone for long.

Sometimes, Connors' mind can control the Lizard's body, but sometimes it is the other way around. Each one tries to overpower the other, and both are always in there somewhere!

While Doctor Connors has long been a
friend of Spider-Man, Professor Miles Warren
missed his chance to become a good friend
of Peter Parker. Instead, the man who
seemed to be just another of Peter's professors
grew to hate both Peter and Spider-Man.
He renamed himself the Jackal, and
dedicated himself to destroying
the wall-crawler – unusually,
by making more of him!

The Jackal blamed
Spider-Man for his own
unhappiness and tricked
other villains into
fighting him. When
he found out that Peter
was Spider-Man, he
used Peter's DNA to
make a clone – an exact
copy of Spidey – to face
the real one in battle.

The pair did
battle, and afterwards
it seemed as if the
clone and the Jackal
had been destroyed
in an explosion.
Yet both of them
had survived, and
when the Jackal
returned, he was able
to convince Peter that the clone was the
real Spider-Man, and that Peter himself
was the copy!

The Jackal made lots more clones
of Peter, and came up with a plan to
give everyone Spider-Man's powers.
He even tried to create a scary new
species of human-spider hybrids.
He has cloned himself many
times, so it is impossible to know
if he is ever really destroyed.

Lots of Spider-Man's enemies are strange, but at least Sandman, Green Goblin, Doc Ock and the others are all still human – even the Lizard is sometimes! Venom, in its natural form, is a shapeless blob that looks more like a liquid than a living being. Only when Venom joins together with a person does it become a vicious Super Villain.

When Peter first encountered Venom, he thought it was just a new material he could use to make a strong Spider-Man costume.

Peter wore the outfit, but realised it was alive and trying to control him. He managed to break away from the alien, but now it knew all of Spider-Man's secrets, and was very angry!

The alien joined with a man called Eddie Brock, who also hated Spider-Man, and the new being called itself Venom. This creature believed it was a hero – and that Spider-Man had to be destroyed.

Venom and Spidey have fought many times, but just when the web-slinger thought he knew how to handle his alien foe, it became more dangerous than ever. No longer linked to Brock's body, it was free to join with other human hosts.

If Venom is the strangest of Spider-Man's foes, then Morlun is the most mysterious. An energy vampire that has lived for hundreds of years, Morlun survives by draining the life-force from people with super powers. For him, Spider-Man is the perfect meal!

Morlun is far stronger than he looks and never shows any sign of tiring. The first time they fought, Spider-Man realised that Morlun would be impossible to defeat with strength alone. He decided that the only thing to do was to give the vampire what he wanted. So he let Morlun feed on him – but only after flooding his own body with a huge dose of radiation.

Spider-Man's powers meant that he was not harmed, but Morlun could not handle so much radioactivity, and he was defeated.

For a time, Spider-Man believed that Morlun had been destroyed once and for all. In fact, Morlun was revived in secret, and continued to hunt for beings with super powers – along with the rest of his mysterious vampire family, the Inheritors.

Now that Morlun has touched Spider-Man in battle, he can find him wherever he goes. Sooner or later, he is sure to return.

Amazing Allies

Peter can always rely on his
friends in times of need – whether
they know him as a Super Hero,
a scientist or the closest thing they will
ever have to a son.

It is Aunt May, of course, who worries
about Peter as if he were her own child –
even though she doesn't know that he is
Spider-Man! In fact, only a handful of
people do know
Peter's secret.

Mary Jane "MJ" Watson has been Peter's friend for many years and worked out for herself that he was Spider-Man. She will always keep his secret and has stood by him during tough times. It's hard work sharing Peter's double life, though, and MJ eventually chose to end their friendship so that she could get on with her own life.

Clever scientist Anna Maria Marconi also uncovered Peter's secret. She worked with Peter and the two of them became good friends. After Anna Maria saw a picture of Spider-Man with marks on his body that matched Peter's, she realised the truth. Now the pair run Parker Industries together.

Peter's Super Hero friendships can be even more complicated than those he shares with his loved ones! Consider the example of cat burglar Felicia Hardy, also known as the Black Cat. She started out as Spider-Man's criminal enemy, then turned her back on burglary to become his girlfriend, but is now his sworn enemy again!

Felicia's father had been a famous cat burglar before her, and she had lived an unhappy life ever since he was caught and sent to prison when she was still a child.

She met Spider-Man on the night that she tried to break her father out of jail. Felicia saw that Spider-Man was not so very different from her – except that he wore a

disguise and worked alone in order to fight crime, not to commit it.

Peter saw that there was a good person behind the Black Cat mask, and tried to help her change her ways. They began to battle bad guys together, and became boyfriend and girlfriend – although Felicia was always more interested in Spider-Man than she was in Peter!

The relationship didn't last, and Felicia has since returned to a life of crime. Though she still has some feelings for Spider-Man, she is now out to destroy him.

DAILY BUGLE ONLINE

SPIDER-MAN FOILS
PRISON BREAK

 PUBLISHED 6 MINUTES AGO 17 COMMENTS SHARE

Spider-Man clashed with the Super Villain known as the Black Cat last night, during an attempted breakout at Ryker's Island maximum security prison.

The notorious cat burglar appears to be the mastermind behind the attempt, judging by security camera footage seen by the *Daily Bugle*.

In the recording, Spider-Man can be seen fighting with the Black Cat before trying to reason with her. He then allows her to flee the scene before special weapons police officers arrive to restore order.

A member of staff at the prison who did not want to be named said: "If Spider-Man hadn't arrived when he did, the breakout would definitely have been a success. We owe him our thanks, but I don't know why he let the Black Cat go".

Spider-Man was unavailable for comment at time of publication.

OSCORP
ADVANCEMENT IN SCIENCE

Above: CCTV footage shows Spider-Man under attack from the Black Cat.

Related stories:

Green is the new black: get the Goblin look

10 things you never knew about Captain America

Why the Black Cat is still at large – inside scoop!

This one weird tip will stop you Hulking out

One of Spider-Man's closest Super Hero friends has been billionaire businessman Tony Stark, who doesn't make any secret of his other identity as Iron Man. Just like the web-slinger himself, Tony is an incredibly gifted scientist, and Peter had always looked up to him as an inspiration.

Tony knows that Peter is Spider-Man, and after their paths crossed several times, he knew he could rely on the younger hero. He invited Peter to live in Stark Tower, and offered him a job as his personal assistant.

Tony became Peter's mentor, offering him his take on being a Super Hero. He also made him a suit of armour that looked a lot like Iron Man's! When war broke out between two groups of Super Heroes, Spider-Man had to choose a side. At first, he stood alongside Iron Man, but ended up fighting him instead.

When the war was over, Super Heroes on both sides felt bad about the harm their fighting had caused. They tried to forget their differences and work together again. Peter still sees Iron Man as an important ally, but will not easily call Tony his friend again.

Iron Man is also a vital member of the greatest Super Hero team ever assembled: the Avengers. Spider-Man has fought alongside the Avengers many times, joining forces with Captain America, Thor, Black Widow, Hawkeye and the Hulk to battle forces that no one hero could beat alone.

Despite their adventures together, the Avengers have not always called Spider-Man a full member of their team. Spidey often prefers to fight alone, and the Avengers do not always agree with how he does things. But when he is really needed, Peter is proud to call himself an Avenger – and they are always happy to help him, too.

When Peter has to rebuild his life after Doc Ock tries to replace him, the Avengers stand by their friend. Captain America and Peter agree that, no matter what, he will always be an Avenger.

AVENGERS CHARTER

We, the Avengers, have banded together to protect the planet Earth, its inhabitants and its resources from any and all threats that might prove to be beyond the power of conventional forces.

As an Avenger, I will dedicate myself to the establishment, growth and preservation of:

- Peace
- Liberty
- Equality
- Justice

Recent global threat: Ultron

This is my solemn oath.

Signed:

Peter Parker

Witnessed by:

Tony Stark   *Steve Rogers*

CONFIDENTIAL

TEAM MEMBERS

As an Avenger, you will make new enemies, but you will also make new friends. Memorise the following names and details before destroying this document.

Steve Rogers   Natalia Romanova   Me!

CAPTAIN AMERICA is a fearless leader. Exposure to Super-Soldier serum has given him enhanced strength, speed and healing powers.

IRON MAN is the genius inventor Tony Stark in a high-tech suit of armour. The suit enables him to fly and use many built-in weapons.

BLACK WIDOW is an expert martial artist and a former spy. A version of the Super-Soldier serum keeps her in peak physical condition.

HAWKEYE is an expert archer whose arrows never miss. He doesn't have any super powers, but is skilled in many martial arts.

THOR is an immortal warrior from the realm of Asgard. His indestructible hammer allows him to fly and travel between dimensions.

THE HULK was created in a nuclear accident. He is incredibly strong and fast, can leap huge distances and is very, very angry.

Call him "Keith"...   Clint Barton   Bruce Banner

Peter, I've written everyone's real names on here, too! - Tony

Spider-Man is also a member of the New Avengers. This team formed to fill the gap that was left behind when the Avengers chose to go their separate ways. But when Captain America brought the Avengers back together, he asked Luke Cage to keep the New Avengers going as an independent team of Super Heroes.

Luke, a very powerful Super Hero with almost unbreakable skin, saw Spider-Man as an obvious choice for his line-up – not least because Spidey had been a part of the team from the beginning. It was not long before Luke and Peter were calling on Ms. Marvel, Mockingbird and Iron Fist to be part of their crimefighting collective.

When Luke left the New Avengers, he stayed good friends with Peter. When they worked together again, it was as part of a new team – the Mighty Avengers!

Great Responsibilities

Life as Spider-Man is never
dull, but some days are much
more challenging than others.
Spidey's greatest adventures have seen him
tested to the limit – fighting against old
friends, and struggling to survive against
seemingly unstoppable foes.

One of the biggest events
to shake Spidey's world was
the Superhuman Civil War.
The war turned friends
into enemies, divided the
Avengers team, and saw
Spider-Man's identity
revealed to the world.
It began with a new
law that meant all
Super Heroes had
to tell the United
States government
who they really were.

Tony Stark made no secret of the fact that he was Iron Man, and he thought the Superhuman Registration Act was a good idea. Tony had helped Peter through some hard times and built him a high-tech new spider suit, so Spider-Man stood alongside Iron Man to support the new law. He even took his mask off in front of a huge crowd to show the whole world who he was.

However, not every Super Hero thought the new law was a good idea. Captain America spoke out against it – and was immediately declared to be an outlaw.

Captain America believed that the Superhuman Registration Act put Super Heroes and their families in unnecessary danger. Some Super Heroes agreed and joined with him to fight against the new law. Soon, other heroes sided with Iron Man and started to hunt down the so-called outlaws.

As the two sides began to fight, Peter saw that he had been wrong to reveal his true identity. If every Super Villain knew that Spider-Man was really Peter Parker, then all the people he loved were now in terrible danger!

Peter turned his back on Iron Man and joined Captain America. It seemed like the fighting would never end, but then Captain America made the most heroic decision of the entire war – he gave up the fight so that no one else would get hurt. Iron Man had won the war, but lost many of his friends.

After the Civil War, Tony Stark learned the dangers of sharing Super Heroes' secrets with the world, and the law was overturned. The magical Doctor Strange made the world forget that Peter was Spider-Man, so his secret identity was safe once more.

THE DIVIDE

When battle lines were drawn between top Avengers, other Super Heroes had to pick a side. Would they support the rule of law with Iron Man, or fight for the freedom to choose alongside Captain America?

CAPTAIN AMERICA
Cap's real name is Steve Rogers, but he believes it is his right to keep that information private if he wants to!

LUKE CAGE
Super-strong Luke goes by his real name, but he believes in the right for everyone to make that choice for themselves.

WICCAN
Billy Kaplan and the other Young Avengers stood with Cap, but they were arrested by Iron Man's forces.

INVISIBLE WOMAN
Sue Richards joined Cap after Iron Man and her husband, Mr. Fantastic, made a dangerous clone of Thor to fight for them.

IRON MAN
The world knows that Tony Stark is Iron Man. He thinks people would be safer if Super Heroes didn't keep secrets.

MS. MARVEL
Before donning her new costume and becoming Captain Marvel, loyal U.S. Air Force officer Carol Danvers backed her government in support of registration.

SHE-HULK
Jennifer Walters is a brilliant lawyer as well as a Super Hero. She believes that all laws should be obeyed.

MR. FANTASTIC
Genius inventor Reed Richards built a Super Hero prison during the Civil War, as well as a violent clone of Thor.

After the Civil War ended, the Avengers reunited to fight Doc Ock and his Super Villain gang, the Sinister Six. Doc Ock convinced the world that he had found a way to stop global warming using special missiles. In reality, he wanted to destroy the planet, leaving just a few survivors to rule over.

When the Avengers tried to stop Ock's plan, he used robots called Octobots to take over their bodies. Only Black Widow and Spider-Man were able to escape. A furious Doc Ock told the world's armies that they would have to destroy Spider-Man to stop global warming.

With the whole world turned against Spider-Man, Peter had to call on allies from the ends of the Earth. He enlisted enough Super Hero friends to launch attacks on all of Doc Ock's missile factories, but the main Avengers were still controlled by Octobots.

Spidey convinced Mysterio to betray the rest of the Sinister Six and help him to save the world. The Super Villain freed the Avengers – allowing them to help Spider-Man destroy the missiles and defeat the Sinister Six.

After his failure to destroy the world, Doctor Octopus did succeed in destroying Peter Parker, seemingly forever.

Using an Octobot to replace Peter's mind with his own, Doc Ock began a new life inside Spidey's body. He called himself the Superior Spider-Man, because he thought he could use Peter's powers better than Peter could!

As Spider-Man, Doc Ock tried to continue his criminal ways – even forming a new Sinister Six team. However, he was surprised to find himself doing heroic things, too. This was because Peter's mind still existed deep inside him. Ock even fell in love with Anna Maria Marconi. When she ended up in danger, he realised that Peter was the only one who could save her. He gave up his control of Spidey, and admitted that Peter really was the best Spider-Man.

World of Spiders

Spider-Man has inspired his fair share of imitators over the years. Some are out to do good, but others use their spider skills for evil.

When the Jackal made a perfect copy of Spider-Man, the real Spidey fought him (see p.50). Everyone thought the clone was destroyed, but when Aunt May was unwell, two Peter Parkers turned up to visit her!

The clone had come back because he had all the same memories as the real Peter. He wanted to do good and called himself Ben Reilly – or the Scarlet Spider when he was in his very own spider suit.

Peter began to think of Ben as a brother. The Green Goblin even convinced Peter that Ben was the real Spidey and Peter was the clone. Ben fought the Goblin, but was turned to dust – which proved to Peter that Ben had been the clone all along.

After Ben, another clone of Peter called Kaine became the Scarlet Spider. He struggled to live a good life as a clone, but eventually became a hero.

Thirteen years after he became Spider-Man, Peter met someone who was bitten by the same spider as he was. Cindy Moon has similar powers to Peter, but can also shoot webs straight from her fingertips. She hid herself away for years to avoid Morlun (see p.54), but Spider-Man rescued her when he thought Morlun was dead. Cindy took the Super Hero name Silk and has since helped Spidey battle villains such as Electro – and the very much alive Morlun!

While Cindy Moon spent years waiting to become Silk, Jessica Drew was destined to be Spider-Woman since before she was born. Her parents were both scientists working with spiders and radiation, and their lab tests affected their unborn child.

Jessica grew up to have super strength and speed, and was tricked into joining the criminal gang Hydra. Yet Spider-Woman rejected life as a Super Villain to become a private detective.

She went on to join the Avengers, and fought alongside Spider-Man in the battle against Morlun.

Not every spider-like being is as friendly as Spider-Man. The creature known as Carnage is an alien version of Peter, formed when a drop of ooze from Venom touched a man called Cletus Kasady. Cletus was a violent criminal even before he was transformed, but with a dose of the Venom alien inside him, he gained its hatred of Spidey, too.

Since Venom used to be linked with Spider-Man, Carnage looks like a twisted take on the Super Hero and can create his own weird webs. Spider-Man has clashed with Carnage many times, and even joined forces with Venom to defeat him. No matter how often Carnage is overcome, he always comes back to cause more chaos.

The villain known as Spider-Slayer did not share any of Spidey's powers but spent his life trying to beat him. The son of a scientist who built "spider slaying" machines, Alastair Smythe wore a robotic suit so that he could become the Ultimate Spider-Slayer.

His fight against Spidey ended when he made the mistake of attacking the Superior Spider-Man, also known as Doctor Octopus.

Doc Ock did not have Spidey's mercy, and so the Spider-Slayer was destroyed.

SPIDER-VERSE HEROES

The Multiverse is home to many versions of planet Earth. Some are very similar to our own, and some are very different, but almost every one has its own version of Spider-Man.

SPIDER-UK
Name: Billy Braddock
Home world: Earth-833
Every version of Earth has a hero to guard the Multiverse. In Peter's world, it is Captain Britain. On Earth-833, it was Spider-UK.

ULTIMATE SPIDER-MAN
Name: Miles Morales
Home world: Earth-1610
A spider that had been injected with a compound containing Peter Parker's blood bit Miles, giving him superhuman powers.

SPIDER-MAN INDIA
Name: Pravitr Prabhakar
Home world: Earth-50101
Pavitr protects the Indian city of Mumbai using spider powers given to him by a mysterious old man.

SPIDER-GWEN
Name: Gwen-Stacey
Home world: Earth-65
In Peter's world, Gwen Stacey was once his girlfriend, but on Earth-65, she is the one who has spider powers!

SP//DR
Name: Peni Parker
Home world: Unknown
Peni allowed herself to be bitten by a radioactive spider so that she could control a special suit of spider armour.

COSMIC SPIDER-MAN
Name: Peter Parker
Home world: Earth-13
This version of Peter Parker gained extra powers from a mysterious outer-space entity called the Enigma Force.

SPIDER-MAN 2099
Name: Miguel O'Hara
Home world: Earth-928
Miguel is a scientist from the year 2099. His world is a future version of Peter Parker's own Earth.

When Spidey learned that Morlun was
still alive, he joined forces with spider Super
Heroes from other realities. Morlun and the
Inheritors could cross the barriers between
universes, so the only way to fight them was
for Spidey to do the same. He visited other
versions of Earth and found that each one
had its own version of Spider-Man – some
of which were very different from him.
The other Spideys wanted Peter to become
their leader, because he was the only one of
them who had ever defeated an Inheritor.

Spider-Man, Silk, Spider-Woman and the assembled heroes of the "Spider-verse" did battle with the Inheritors across many different worlds. In their final showdown, Morlun was defeated when Spidey sent him to a world where the radiation was strong enough to sap his powers.

Soon, all the Inheritors were banished to this radioactive prison. The brave spider heroes all went back to their own realities, leaving Earth once more in the care of its friendly neighbourhood Spider-Man.

Quiz

1. What is the first name of Peter Parker's aunt?

2. What power lets Peter know when danger is near?

3. How much weight can Spider-Man lift?

4. John Jonah Jameson hired Peter as a photographer for which newspaper?

5. What is the name of the company where Peter is the boss?

6. What is the Green Goblin's real name?

7. What is the name of Doc Ock's gang?

8. What is the full name of Peter's friend MJ?

9. Who made Peter a suit of armour similar
    to Iron Man's?

10. What gives Captain America his powers?

11. Which Super Villain told the world he could
    stop global warming?

12. What is Jennifer Walters'
    Super Hero name?

13. True or false: Silk uses web
    shooters like Spider-Man's.

14. Who was the Spider-Slayer?

15. How is Miguel O'Hara
    better known?

See page 92 for answers.

Glossary

Absorb
Soak up one thing inside another, like water in a sponge.

Cat burglar
A thief that moves as carefully and as quietly as a cat.

Clone
An exact copy of a person or thing.

Encouraged
Gave help and support.

Glimpse
A quick look.

Government
A group of people allowed to make laws and rules.

Havoc
Destruction and disorder.

Hijack
To take control of something without permission.

Hybrid
A mix of two different things.

Indestructible
Something that can't be destroyed.

Inspiration
A thing or person that influences you or sparks ideas for you.

Laboratory
A place where scientists work, also called a lab.

Mentor
Someone who gives training and advice.

Outlaw
Someone living in a way that goes against the law.

Puny
Small and weak.

Radioactivity
A kind of energy that can be very dangerous in large amounts.

Reflexes
Actions your body make without thinking.

Reptiles
Animals with cold blood and scaly skin, such as snakes.

Responsibility
A job that you have to do.

Sinister
Creepy and evil.

Vibration
Very fast shaking movements.

Quiz answers
1. May 2. Spider-sense
3. Almost 10 tonnes
4. Daily Bugle 5. Parker
Industries 6. Norman Osborn
7. The Sinister Six
8. Mary Jane Watson 9. Tony Stark 10. Super-Soldier serum
11. Doc Ock 12. She-Hulk
13. False – she can shoot webs from her fingertips 14. Alastair Smythe 15. Spider-Man 2099

Index

Guide for Parents

DK Reads is a three-level interactive reading adventure series for children, developing the habit of reading widely for both pleasure and information. These chapter books have an exciting main narrative interspersed with a range of reading genres to suit your child's reading ability, as required by the National Curriculum. Each book is designed to develop your child's reading skills, fluency, grammar awareness, and comprehension in order to build confidence and engagement when reading.

Ready for a *Reading Alone* book
YOUR CHILD SHOULD

- be able to read independently and silently for extended periods of time.
- read aloud flexibly and fluently, in expressive phrases with the listener in mind.
- respond to what they are reading with an enquiring mind.

A Valuable and Shared Reading Experience

Supporting children when they are reading proficiently can encourage them to value reading and to view reading as an interesting, purposeful and enjoyable pastime. So here are a few tips on how to use this book with your child.

TIP 1 Reading aloud as a learning opportunity:

- If your child has already read some of the book, ask him/her to explain the earlier part briefly.
- Encourage your child to read slightly slower than his/her normal silent reading speed so that the words are clear and the listener has time to absorb the information, too.

Reading aloud provides your child with practice in expressive reading and performing to a listener, as well as a chance to share his/her responses to the storyline and the information.

TIP 2 Praise, share and chat:

• Encourage your child to recall specific details after each chapter.

• Provide opportunities for your child to pick out interesting words and discuss what they mean.

• Discuss how the author captures the reader's interest, or how effective the non-fiction layouts are.

• Ask the questions provided on some pages and in the quiz. These help to develop comprehension skills and awareness of the language used.

• Ask if there's anything that your child would like to discover more about.

Further information can be researched in the index of other non-fiction books or on the Internet.

A FEW ADDITIONAL TIPS

• Continue to read to your child regularly to demonstrate fluency, phrasing and expression; to find out or check information; and for sharing enjoyment.

• Encourage your child to read a range of different genres, such as newspapers, poems, review articles and instructions.

• Provide opportunities for your child to read to a variety of eager listeners, such as a sibling or a grandparent.

Have you read these other great books from DK?

III **READING ALONE** III

 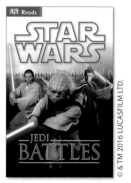

Read all about
the scariest
monsters in the
Star Wars galaxy.

Join the mighty
Avengers as they
battle the power-
mad robot Ultron!

Find out all about
the brave Jedi
Knights and their
epic adventures.

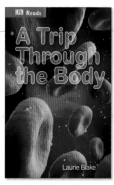

Discover how to
survive in the most
hostile place on
Earth – Antarctica.

Enjoy the myths
and legends from
long ago and
across the world.

Explore the
amazing systems
at work inside the
human body.